For my sweet Billy,
remembering with love all the great
cities we wandered in together

SIMON & SCHUSTER BOOKS FOR YOUNG READERS
An imprint of Simon & Schuster Children's Publishing Division
1230 Avenue of the Americas, New York, New York 10020
© 2023 by Anita Lobel
Book design by Laurent Linn © 2023 by Simon & Schuster, Inc.
SIMON & SCHUSTER BOOKS FOR YOUNG READERS and related marks
are trademarks of Simon & Schuster, Inc.
For information about special discounts for bulk purchases,
please contact Simon & Schuster Special Sales at 1-866-506-1949
or business@simonandschuster.com.
The Simon & Schuster Speakers Bureau can bring authors to your live event.
For more information or to book an event, contact the Simon & Schuster Speakers Bureau
at 1-866-248-3049 or visit our website at www.simonspeakers.com.
The text for this book was set in Acta Book.
The illustrations for this book were rendered in gouache with pencil and liquid ink pen.
Manufactured in China
1022 SCP
First Edition
2 4 6 8 10 9 7 5 3 1
Library of Congress Cataloging-in-Publication Data
Names: Lobel, Anita, author, illustrator.
Title: Good morning, good night / Anita Lobel.
Description: First edition. | New York : Simon & Schuster Books for Young Readers, 2023 |
"A Paula Wiseman book." | Audience: Ages 4–8. |
Audience: Grades K–1. | Summary: A family's day spent in the city
reveals a wealth of contrasting images.
Identifiers: LCCN 2022007385 (print) | LCCN 2022007386 (ebook) |
ISBN 9781534465947 (hardcover) | ISBN 9781534465954 (ebook)
Subjects: CYAC: City and town life–Fiction. | Opposites–Fiction. |
Families–Fiction. | LCGFT: Picture books.
Classification: LCC PZ7.L7794 Go 2023 (print) | LCC PZ7.L7794 (ebook) | DDC [E]–dc23
LC record available at https://lccn.loc.gov/2022007385
LC ebook record available at https://lccn.loc.gov/2022007386

GOOD
MORNING,

GOOD
NIGHT

ANITA LOBEL

A PAULA WISEMAN BOOK
SIMON & SCHUSTER BOOKS FOR YOUNG READERS
NEW YORK LONDON TORONTO SYDNEY NEW DELHI

Good Morning!

Good Morning?

NOT YET.

I am awake.
I want to be out. I want to walk. I want to look and see.

Mama and Papa promised to be up and ready.
But they are asleep. And dreaming. And snoring.
I eat half a banana.

I am bored!

I brush my teeth.

I comb my hair.

I button my shirt.

I put on my shoes.

I am bored!

But then . . .

the sun is rising.
Mama and Papa are waking.

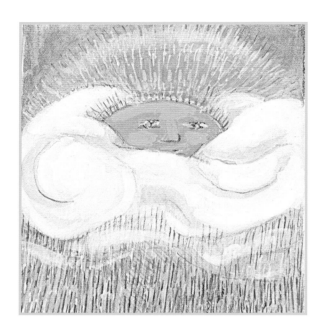 

"Good morning," mumbles Mama.
"Good morning," mumbles Papa.

They splash in the shower.
They drink coffee.
They smell good.

At last!
They are dressed.

"Are we ready to be out and about?" asks Papa.
"Are we ready to look and see?" asks Mama.
They don't know I have been ready for a long time.
"YES," I say. "Yes! I am! Very, very, very ready."

We see a **little** dog
step out of a door in a house.

We watch a large workman
climb out of a hole in the street.

Look up there! A **big** bird
is hovering high above a column.

See down here! Tiny birds
are pecking below a fire hydrant.

We look at the **calm** ceramic cat
sitting still on a windowsill.

We watch a **fierce** live cat
chasing his prey on the sidewalk.

Aah! Smell the fresh flowers
in vases.

Ooh! Admire the painted flowers
in pictures.

Smile at the fancy, **brand-new** shoes
displayed in the store window.

Be sorry for the broken, **worn-out** shoes
thrown out by the garbage.

Phi, phi! Listen to the **thin whistles**
of the piccolo.

Hrum, hrum. Hear the **round growls**
of the bass.

Hush! Don't disturb the old people dozing.

Ssh! Don't wake the new baby snoozing.

Spicy hot dogs with mustard.
Yum!

Sweet ice cream and soda.
More yum!

No! That **hard** chair
might not be nice to sit on.

Yes! This **soft** chair
would be very nice to sink into.

We wait for the train
roaring below the city street.

We walk on the bridge
under arches soaring above us.

Now we are home.
The day, which was not boring at all, has come and gone.
I am happy. I am sleepy.

I will dream of morning that will wake me tomorrow,
to begin a new day.

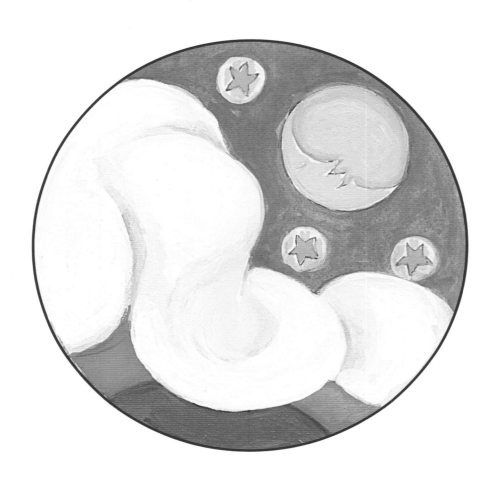